The Tale of Major Monkey

Arthur Scott Bailey

The Tale of Major Monkey

I

Strange Whispers

The wild folk in Pleasant Valley were whispering strange stories to one another. If the stories were true, they were most amazing. And if they were merely made up to cause talk, certainly they succeeded.

Perhaps if somebody less tricky than Peter Mink and Tommy Fox had started these odd tales, the rest of the wild folk might have been quicker to believe them.

Anyhow, the news offered the best of excuses for gossip. And many of the field- and forest-people repeated it so often that they almost began to believe it themselves.

All but old Mr. Crow. He declared stoutly that the whole thing was nothing but a hoax.

"You can't fool me!" he told people. But when they said that they had no intention of trying to, he had to change his statement. "I mean"—he explained—"I mean that neither Tommy Fox nor Peter Mink can fool me. They can't make me believe that they've seen anybody hanging by his tail in a tree-top."

"Why not?" asked Mr. Crow's cousin, Jasper Jay.

"Becaws——" said Mr. Crow. And then he corrected himself once more. "Because," he replied, "no 'possum ever came so far North as this. I've spent a good many winters in the South, and I ought to know. And besides," he added, "although a 'possum can hang by his tail, there never was one that could throw a stick or a stone. And I ought to know, for I've spent a good many winters in the South, where the 'possums live."

Everybody had to admit that old Mr. Crow must know what he was talking about. And people began to feel rather foolish when they realized how near they had been to letting those two rascals—Peter Mink and Tommy Fox—deceive them.

As for old Mr. Crow, having persuaded his neighbors to his way of thinking, he began to be more pleased with himself than ever. And he spent a good deal of time sitting in a tall tree near the cornfield, with his head on one side, hoping that his friends would notice how wise he looked.

He was engaged in that agreeable pastime one afternoon when—thump!—something struck the limb on which he was perched.

Mr. Crow gave a squawk and a jump. And then he glanced quickly toward the ground.

There was no one anywhere in sight. So Mr. Crow looked somewhat silly. For a moment he had thought that Johnnie Green had thrown something at him. But he saw at once that he was mistaken. Of course it could have been nothing more than a dead branch falling.

He settled himself again, trying to appear as if he hadn't been startled, when—plump!—something gave him a smart blow on his back.

Old Mr. Crow flopped hastily into a neighboring tree. And this time he looked up instead of down.

At first he could see nothing unusual. And he had almost made up his mind that something had fallen out of the sky, when a head showed itself from behind a limb and a queer, wrinkled face peered at him.

Mr. Crow did not recognize the face. It was an odd one. In fact, he thought he had never seen an odder. But if he thought the face a queer one, it was not half as peculiar as the stranger's actions.

For, as Mr. Crow watched him, the stranger slipped into full view, hanging by his tail and one hand from a limb, while with the other hand he waved a red cap.

Old Mr. Crow's mouth fell open. For a time he said never a word.

And for him, that was quite out of the ordinary.

3

II

No 'Possum

At first old Mr. Crow could scarcely believe his eyes. He stared and stared. Certainly it was no 'possum that he saw. And yet the stranger was hanging by his tail.

There could be no doubt about that. Even as Mr. Crow watched him he waved both hands at Mr. Crow, and swung by his tail alone.

The old gentleman was terribly upset. During all the summers he had spent in Pleasant Valley he had never seen any such person there before.

For a moment Mr. Crow was worried about himself. He wondered if he was not ill. He knew he had eaten a good deal of corn that day. And he half hoped that that was the trouble—that perhaps he saw something that wasn't really in the tree at all.

Then he remembered the blow on his back. Had the queer person in the tree-top struck him?... Mr. Crow grew angry.

"Did you hit me?" he called.

"I'm not sure," said the stranger. "But I think I did, for I saw you jump."

"Then you threw something at me!" Mr. Crow screamed.

"Oh, no!" the other replied. "I didn't throw anything at you, sir. I merely dropped something on your back."

Mr. Crow choked. Perhaps it was as well that he could not speak just then. He coughed and spluttered and swallowed and swayed back and forth, trying to get his breath. And he had begun, at last to feel better, when— biff!—something struck him again and all but knocked him over.

The stranger gave a shrill whistle.

"I threw something that time!" he jeered.

Old Mr. Crow felt that he had been terribly insulted. He looked as dignified as he could. And he would have turned his back on the stranger—had he dared.

While he was wondering whether he had better fly away, or stay and quarrel with the rude person who had pelted him, the boorish stranger leaped from the tall tree into the smaller one where Mr. Crow was sitting. Then, dropping nimbly from limb to limb, with the help of his hands and his feet and his tail, he stopped at last when he had reached Mr. Crow's level.

One thing was certain. The stranger was bold as brass. He looked Mr. Crow up and down. And then he said:

"You're a gay old bird! What's your name?"

Now, no doubt some people would have been angry. But Mr. Crow rather liked to be called gay, because he couldn't help looking solemn. And most people knew he was very old. And everybody was aware he was a bird. So he said hoarsely:

"My name is Mister Crow—and please don't forget the Mister."

The stranger put on his flat-topped red cap and touched the visor smartly with his right hand, in a military manner.

Old Mr. Crow couldn't help admiring the newcomer's clothes. He wore a red coat trimmed with gold braid, and bright blue trousers.

"That's a handsome suit that you have on," Mr. Crow observed. "I shouldn't mind having one like it myself."

The stranger seemed pleased. And he touched his cap again.

"I'm afraid you can't have a suit like this," he said. "It's a uniform—that's what it is. And, of course, a plain Mister like you can't wear a uniform. But I wear one because I'm a soldier."

Old Mr. Crow was disappointed. But he soon brightened up. Though he wasn't a soldier himself, at least it was pleasant to know one. So he decided to forget that he had been angry with the stranger.

"What's your name?" he asked.

"Major Monkey," said the newcomer, knocking off his cap with one hand and catching it with the other as it fell. "When you speak to me, please don't forget the Major," he added.

III

Getting Acquainted

Major Monkey and old Mr. Crow had a long talk. They got on famously together, because the old gentleman liked to pry into other people's affairs and the Major loved to talk about himself.

In reply to Mr. Crow's questions, Major Monkey explained that he was a great traveller. And having found himself in the village a few miles away, he had taken a notion to see the surrounding country.

"This is a delightful spot," the Major remarked. "And if your neighbors are half as pleasant as you are, I think I'll stay right here for the present."

Naturally, old Mr. Crow was flattered. He couldn't remember when anybody had said he was pleasant.

"I hope you will settle in Pleasant Valley," he told Major Monkey. "As for the neighbors — well, you'll find them a queer lot, mostly."

"What's the matter with them?" the Major asked him.

Thereupon old Mr. Crow shook his head.

"They're not at all like me," he replied slowly.

"Of course, there's my cousin, Jasper Jay. He's not a bad sort — except that he's rude, noisy, and a good deal of a rascal. But the others — well, most of them are too greedy. If I didn't watch this cornfield closely some of them wouldn't care if they didn't leave a single kernel for anybody else."

"Do you like corn?" the Major inquired.

Mr. Crow swallowed once or twice before answering.

"I can eat it," he said finally. "It keeps one alive, you know. But if you've never had any, I advise you not to touch it."

Major Monkey thanked him.

"Don't mention it!" said Mr. Crow. "I'm delighted to be of help to a stranger. And if there is anything else I can do, don't hesitate to call on me."

7

Major Monkey thanked him again. And then he said:

"I'd like to get acquainted with all the neighbors—such as they are. And I would suggest that you give a party and invite me and a lot of people to come to it, so I can meet them."

Old Mr. Crow bit his tongue. It struck him that Major Monkey was just the least bit too forward.

"What about refreshments?" Mr. Crow asked him. "It's easy to see that you don't know the neighbors. I can tell you that they have enormous appetites—every one of them."

"Oh! that's easily arranged," said Major Monkey. "Tell everybody to be sure to have his refreshments before he comes to the party."

"A good idea!" Mr. Crow exclaimed. With that difficulty removed he was willing to give a party, for he quite liked the prospect of introducing everybody to "his old friend, Major Monkey."

"You're sure you don't know anybody in this valley except me?" Mr. Crow asked. He didn't want to divide with anyone else the honor of being a friend of anybody so imposing as the Major.

"I haven't spoken to a soul but you," Major Monkey assured him.

Mr. Crow said he was glad of that. And then he asked the Major to keep out of sight until the time came for the party to begin.

At first Major Monkey objected. And not until Mr. Crow promised to have the party that very day—an hour before sunset—did he consent to hide himself.

"Where's a good place?" he asked Mr. Crow.

"That tree is hollow," said Mr. Crow, pointing to the one in which he had first seen the Major. "Just slip inside that hole there, about half way up the trunk, and don't come out till I call you!"

Major Monkey scrambled back into the tall tree. And Mr. Crow watched him narrowly until he was out of sight. Indeed, the old gentleman even continued to stare at the hole after his friend had vanished inside it.

IV

Wanted — A Lodging

Afterward old Mr. Crow had to admit that he must have been forgetful. He had told Major Monkey to hide inside the hollow tree. And being a total stranger in the neighborhood, of course the Major didn't know that an owl lived there.

So he entered the dark hole boldly. And soon he came dashing out of it much faster than he had gone in, shrieking at the top of his voice.

Old Mr. Crow was poised on a branch, as if he were waiting for something. And he almost smiled as he looked at the Major and saw that he was shaking. The poor fellow's teeth were chattering, too.

"What's the matter?" Mr. Crow called to him.

"There's — there's a Tiger inside this tree!" Major Monkey stammered. "I know it's a Tiger, for I saw his eyes."

"Nonsense!" Mr. Crow exclaimed. And he burst into a loud haw-haw. "It's nothing but an old Owl. I forgot all about him. A fine soldier you are — afraid of an old Owl!"

Major Monkey straightened his cap and looked as soldierly as he could.

"You're mistaken, in a way," he told Mr. Crow. "I admit I was afraid. I was afraid I had frightened him, waking him up so suddenly. So I retreated."

Old Mr. Crow stopped laughing and looked very thoughtful. It occurred to him that Major Monkey was a somewhat slippery person. Certainly he could slip out of a hole about as easily as anybody Mr. Crow knew.

"You'll have to find some other place for me to hide," the Major announced. "I don't want to stay in this tree all day, for I shouldn't like to disturb a gentleman's rest."

Mr. Crow pondered for a few moments.

"You see that old haystack?" he said at last, pointing across the fields. "Go and burrow under that. And be back here exactly an hour before sunset."

Major Monkey saluted.

"That suits me," he said. And then he turned and scurried down to the ground, leaped quickly upon the fence, and galloped off along the topmost rails.

Mr. Crow spent a very busy day inviting everybody to his party, to meet his old friend, Major Monkey.

"He's a famous soldier," Mr. Crow explained, when people asked him questions. "And I hope you'll all wear your best clothes, because the Major himself is very handsomely dressed. There's gold braid on his coat, and on his cap, too."

The old gentleman talked so much about the Major's uniform that a good many of the neighbors thought that Mr. Crow ought to postpone his party for a few days, until they could get Mr. Frog, the tailor, to make them some new clothes.

But Mr. Crow wouldn't listen to them.

"No!" he said. "We mustn't wait. My friend the Major is a great traveller. There's no knowing when he will take it into his head to move on. And if you want to meet him there's no time like the present."

Well, people were so busy getting ready for the party that there was a great flurry everywhere all day long—except at the haystack, where Major Monkey was hiding. And even he did not have so dull a time as you might suppose.

Luckily, he had discovered a lone apple tree near-by. And being fond of fruit he crept out of the haystack every few minutes and gathered apples.

What he could eat, he ate greedily. And what he couldn't he hid under the stack.

And on the whole, he had rather a pleasant time.

V

Meeting Major Monkey

Everybody was prompt when the hour came for Mr. Crow's party. In fact, everybody was ahead of time. Old Mr. Crow had talked so much about his old friend Major Monkey and the Major's gold-braided uniform that people simply couldn't wait to see the stranger and his fine clothes.

There was just one difficulty: the Major himself was not on hand.

Old Mr. Crow began to be terribly worried. But he tried not to let anybody know that he was disturbed.

"He'll be here soon," he said when people asked him where Major Monkey was. "I've never known my friend the Major to break an engagement. He's a bit late—that's all. I only hope he isn't lost. You know he's a stranger in these parts."

Now, Mr. Crow was sitting in a tree, gazing toward the haystack in the distance, where he had told the Major to hide. And he had hardly finished speaking when a big red apple struck the tree just above his head with a loud smack and broke into bits.

Mr. Crow jumped. And so did everybody else. But before the party had time to scatter, Major Monkey peeped from behind a neighboring tree and uttered a piercing whistle.

"Don't go, friends!" Mr. Crow cried to his companions. "Here he is now! Here's Major Monkey himself.... That's only one of his jokes," he added, for he noticed that some of his cronies appeared somewhat nervous.

Major Monkey drew nearer. His face bore a wide grin; while in his hand he clutched another red apple, which he threatened playfully to throw at the company.

"Don't do that, Major!" Mr. Crow called. "You might get hungry, you know. And if you do, you can eat that apple."

Major Monkey touched his cap to Mr. Crow. He seemed to think that was good advice, for he lowered the hand that held the apple.

On hearing Mr. Crow's suggestion the whole company began to laugh. They seemed to think that Mr. Crow was joking.

"Who ever heard of anybody going hungry at a party?" Fatty Coon exclaimed. And turning to Mr. Crow, he asked him where the refreshments were.

The old gentleman seemed taken aback.

"I declare," he gasped, "I forgot to tell you all to have your refreshments before you came."

"Isn't there going to be anything to eat?" Fatty Coon asked him anxiously.

Mr. Crow shook his head.

"It really doesn't matter," he said, talking very fast. "You know, I invited everybody to meet my old friend, Major Monkey. And here he is, all ready to tell you about his travels. But first we'll have a little music."

It was now the Major's turn to look uneasy.

"Music!" he echoed. "I hope you haven't gone and got a hand-organ!"

"No—not that!" said Mr. Crow. "The Woodchuck brothers are going to whistle for us."

"Oh!" said the Major, who appeared much relieved. "I was afraid you had a hand-organ. And I don't care for that sort of music. I've heard too much of it on my travels."

At a signal from Mr. Crow, the Woodchuck brothers stepped forward and started to whistle a lively tune, called "Clover Blossoms." Being very fond of clover blossoms, the musicians began whistling in a most spirited fashion. But they had bad luck.

Though he did not know the tune, Major Monkey insisted on whistling, too. And all the company stopped up their ears, except Mr. Crow. He stood the noise as long as he could. And then he ordered the whistlers to stop. "What tune were you whistling?" he asked the Major.

"It's called 'Banana Blossoms,'" Major Monkey explained. "You see, I'm very fond of bananas."

Old Mr. Crow laughed.

"The two tunes don't go well together," he said. "So we won't have any more music."

And Fatty Coon cried that he was glad of that, because when people whistled about things to eat it only made him hungrier than ever.

VI

Too Many Disputes

On the whole, Mr. Crow's party would have been a great success if it hadn't been for Peter Mink and Tommy Fox.

As soon as Major Monkey showed himself, after throwing the apple at Mr. Crow, those two began whispering slyly together. And when the Major climbed a tree and hung from a limb by his tail they both jumped up and said to Mr. Crow:

"We saw Major Monkey before you ever did!"

Mr. Crow promptly flew into a rage.

"You did not!" he squalled.

"Yes, we did!" they declared. "We told people several days ago that we had seen a stranger hanging by his tail; and nobody believed us because you said it wasn't possible. You said nobody but a 'possum could do that, and that no 'possum ever came as far north as Pleasant Valley."

Old Mr. Crow was very angry. Although he knew that Tommy and Peter were speaking the truth, he did not care to hear it. Certainly there was no use of his denying what they said. But an idea popped into his head.

"Which of you saw the Major first?" he asked.

"I did!" they both bawled at the same time. And then followed a terrible dispute: "You didn't! I did! I did! You didn't!"

Now, that was exactly what Mr. Crow wanted. He had started Peter Mink and Tommy Fox to quarreling. "They'll never agree," Mr. Crow cried. "Let's ask Major Monkey to settle the dispute! Let's leave it to him!" And turning to his friend, the Major, Mr. Crow said: "Which of these two sharp-nosed rascals did you see first?"

Major Monkey took a bite out of his apple while he looked closely at Peter Mink and Tommy Fox.

15

"I never saw either of them until I came to this party," he declared. "And then I saw both at the same time, because they were whispering together."

"There!" Mr. Crow shouted to the whole company. "You hear what my old friend the Major says?"

Tommy Fox and Peter Mink stopped quarreling.

"You didn't ask the Major the proper question!" they objected. "We never said he saw us at all! We said — — "

But Mr. Crow waved them aside.

"If you aren't too hungry," he muttered to Major Monkey, "I'd suggest that you let fly with that red apple."

The Major was only too willing. With deadly aim he flung the apple at Peter Mink and Tommy Fox. First it hit Peter on the nose, and then it bounced off and struck Tommy on his nose.

And then the party came to an end in an awful uproar. For Peter and Tommy were very angry. Those that could fly flew away in a great hurry. And those that could run scampered quickly out of sight. As for the soldier, Major Monkey, he climbed a tree and hung by his tail from a limb, where he swung backwards and forwards and made faces at Tommy Fox and Peter Mink until their rage was terrible to see.

Mr. Crow did not desert his friend the Major. He remained in a tree near-by, to watch the fun. And there's no telling how long it would have lasted had not Major Monkey pulled himself suddenly up on a limb and laid a hand across the front of his red coat. There was a look of pain upon his face.

"What's the matter?" Mr. Crow asked him. "Are you wounded?" he inquired. Knowing that the Major was a soldier, he could think of nothing but a wound that would make him act as he did.

"I—I'm not sure," Major Monkey replied. "It may be that I've eaten too many apples."

VII

The Major Has a Pain

The party had come to an end; nobody was left except old Mr. Crow and his friend Major Monkey.

Mr. Crow himself was fast growing sleepy, for it was almost dark. And he wanted to fly home and go to bed. But he hardly felt that he ought to leave just then.

There was no doubt that the Major was in great pain. He kept one hand pressed against the lowest button of his short red coat. His cap was awry. And his wrinkled face showed a careworn and anxious look.

"How many apples have you eaten to-day?" Mr. Crow asked his friend.

"I haven't the slightest idea," the Major answered. "After I had finished two dozen I lost count."

"My goodness!" Mr. Crow exclaimed. "It's no wonder you're ill.... We'll hurry over to the pasture and see Aunt Polly Woodchuck, the herb doctor.She'll know what to do for you."

Major Monkey was more than willing. So they set out at once. The Major travelled through the tree-tops where he could, while Mr. Crow flew slowly, alighting now and then to wait for his friend to overtake him.

In a little while they came to the pasture. And Major Monkey was glad to find Aunt Polly at home.

She was a wise old lady. She knew right away, without being told, that it was Major Monkey—and not Mr. Crow—that was ill.

"You're in pain," she remarked to the Major. "I knew it the moment I set eyes on you."

Major Monkey moaned faintly.

"I hope you'll give me something to make me feel better," he wailed.

"I will," Aunt Polly Woodchuck promised. And putting her hand inside a basket that she carried on her arm, she drew forth a red apple. "Here!" she said, "eat this!"

Major Monkey drew back.

"No!" he groaned. "I don't want any more apples. I've had too many already."

Aunt Polly Woodchuck shot a triumphant look at Mr. Crow.

"I thought so," she said. And she dropped the red apple back into her basket. "Now," she went on, turning again to the Major, "I should like to ask whether you're fond of corn."

Old Mr. Crow stepped forward quickly.

"I object!" he cried. "The less said about corn, the better!"

Aunt Polly Woodchuck hastened to explain that she meant no offense to anyone.

"I merely wondered," she said, "whether you gave your guests corn to eat at your party."

"Certainly not!" Mr. Crow exploded. "Certainly not!" And he glared at the old lady as if to say: "Change the subject—for pity's sake!"

"You're a stranger in these parts, I take it," Aunt Polly said, turning once more to Major Monkey. "No doubt you've been used to eating different food from what you get hereabouts."

"That's so," the Major admitted. "I've been living mostly on boiled rice, with a baked potato now and then."

"Ah! Cooked food!" said Aunt Polly. "And if you had that sort of fare, you must have been living with men."

The Major looked uneasy.

"I don't care to talk about my past," he murmured. "Just you give me something to warm my stomach a bit. That's all I ask of you."

Well, Aunt Polly Woodchuck handed him some peppermint leaves.

"Chew these," she directed him. "And if you don't feel better to-morrow I'll lose my guess."

Major Monkey put the leaves into his mouth and made a wry face.

"Haven't you a lump of sugar to make this dose taste better?" he asked her.

"There!" Aunt Polly cried. "You've been fed by men! I knew it all the time."

Major Monkey made no comment on her remark. And settling his cap firmly on his head he said that he must be going.

So he and Mr. Crow went off.

"Where are you going to spend the night?" Mr. Crow asked him as soon as they were out of Aunt Polly's hearing.

"That haystack is a good place," said the Major. "I believe I'll live there as long as I stay in Pleasant Valley."

"It's not far from the farmhouse," Mr. Crow observed. "Perhaps you could steal—er—I mean find a little cooked food there now and then."

"That's an idea," Major Monkey told him. But he did not explain whether he thought it a good one or not.

VIII

A Secret

When Major Monkey awoke the following morning his pain had left him. Creeping from the haystack where he had slept, he cast longing eyes at the red apples in the tree near-by. But he remembered his trouble of the evening before. And he remembered likewise what Mr. Crow had said about "finding" something to eat at the farmhouse.

But for some reason the Major wanted to avoid Farmer Green's house. To be sure, he would have enjoyed sitting down with the family at the breakfast table. But he was afraid something might prevent his leaving after he had eaten.

Luckily Major Monkey was a person who could usually find a way out of any difficulty. And now he made up his mind that a light meal of eggs was the very thing he needed in order to begin the day right. So he went straight to the woods and climbed the first tree he came to — a pine tree just beyond the fence.

There Major Monkey found exactly what he was looking for. In a warbler's nest, a dozen feet from the ground, he beheld five speckled eggs.

The owners of the nest were not at home. But knowing that one or the other would soon return, the Major did not care to linger long over their treasures.

He noticed that one of the eggs was bigger than the others.

"Really there are too many eggs here for this small nest," the Major said to himself. "If I take the big one I'll be doing the owners a favor."

So he picked up the big egg, and holding it carefully in one hand he hurried away.

When he had put some distance between himself and the nest, Major Monkey stopped to enjoy his breakfast. He was just on the point of opening the egg, when who should come up but old Mr. Crow.

The Major quickly hid his breakfast behind his back.

"Good morning!" said Mr. Crow. "I hope you are feeling better to-day."

"Oh, yes—thank you!" said Major Monkey. "I'm quite well again."

Mr. Crow's sharp eyes pierced him through and through.

"What are you holding behind you?" he asked bluntly.

The Major saw that he was caught.

"It's my breakfast," he confessed, giving Mr. Crow a quick glance at what was in his hand. "I—I found it," he said. "Wasn't I lucky?"

"A bird's egg!" Mr. Crow exclaimed disapprovingly. "What kind is it?"

"It's nothing but a Warbler's egg," Major Monkey replied.

The old gentleman smiled knowingly. And feeling more comfortable, Major Monkey opened his hand and gave Mr. Crow a good look at his prize.

"That's too big for a Warbler's egg!" Mr. Crow cried.

"I found it in a Warbler's nest," Major Monkey insisted.

"Were there any more like this one in the nest?" Mr. Crow asked.

"Oh, yes!" the Major answered.

"Were they as big as this egg?" Mr. Crow inquired.

Major Monkey explained that they were not.

"Just as I supposed!" the old gentleman exclaimed. "This isn't a Warbler's egg. It's a Cowbird's egg. And you've done that Warbler family a good turn by taking it out of their nest.

"I know Mrs. Cowbird," he went on. "She's too lazy to bring up her own children. So she sneaks through the woods and lays her eggs in other folk's nests.... I must tell of this," Mr. Crow added. "People will think very kindly of you when they hear what you have done."

But Major Monkey begged him not to mention the matter to anyone.

He pleaded so hard that at last Mr. Crow consented to keep the affair a secret between them. And Mr. Crow couldn't help thinking that Major Monkey was one of the most modest people he had ever met.

Then the Major opened the egg with great skill, and ate its contents without spilling a drop.

"Now," he said, "now I'm ready for business."

IX

The Major Has a Plan

"What is your business, if I may ask?" Mr. Crow inquired of Major Monkey.

"Lately I've been spending my time travelling," the Major replied. "But you know I'm a soldier. And while I'm in Pleasant Valley I intend to form an army."

Old Mr. Crow looked somewhat worried when he heard that.

"I hope you aren't going to guard the cornfield!" he said hastily.

Major Monkey set his fears at rest.

"We'll let Farmer Green do that," he said with a wink. "This is what we'll do: we'll band ourselves together and we'll fight any strangers that come to Pleasant Valley to live."

"That's not a bad plan," Mr. Crow remarked. "But it's lucky for you that you didn't form the army before you got here yourself—else we'd have had to fight you."

"Of course!" Major Monkey agreed. "But trust me not to make such a mistake as that."

"Who's going to be in the army?" Mr. Crow wanted to know.

"Everybody!" the Major answered, with a wave of the hand that took in the whole valley.

For as long as a minute old Mr. Crow was very thoughtful.

"I shall not care to be in it unless I can be a general," he announced at last.

"Why, certainly!" said Major Monkey. "Certainly you shall be a general, Mr. Crow."

Mr. Crow swelled himself up and looked as important as he could.

"Get everybody to come to the edge of the woods, near the pasture, early to-morrow morning," Major Monkey commanded.

"Aren't you going to do any of the work?" Mr. Crow demanded. "I thought generals didn't have to do anything except look wise."

"It's easier for you to get about than it is for me. But as soon as we have our army together I'll take entire charge of it," Major Monkey informed him.

Mr. Crow was satisfied. After all, it wouldn't really be work, he told himself, to fly around and tell the people the news. In fact, the more he thought about the plan the better he liked it.

So he bade Major Monkey good-by and hurried away.

When Mr. Crow had flown out of sight the Major rolled over and over on the ground. And then he climbed a tree and swung by his tail from a limb, while he made an odd, chuckling sound.

"A general!" he said. "General Crow! Why he never wore a uniform in all his life!"

On the following morning the field-and forest-folk began gathering at the edge of the woods near the pasture almost before it was light. And when Major Monkey left his snug bed in the haystack and went to the meeting-place he found an eager throng waiting for him.

Old Mr. Crow was flitting about, talking in a loud voice, and ordering people around to his heart's content.

"Silence!" Major Monkey commanded, as soon as he arrived. Mr. Crow opened his mouth to speak. But Major Monkey cut him off short.

"The first thing a soldier has to learn is to obey," he barked.

"But I'm a general!" Mr. Crow protested.

"Well, these are general orders; so you'll have to obey 'em," said Major Monkey glibly.

And poor old Mr. Crow didn't know what to say to that.

But he couldn't help looking rather grumpy.

X

The New Army

"Now, then—fall in!" Major Monkey shouted to the whole company of field-and forest-folk.

But nobody had the slightest idea what he meant.

"You don't suppose he expects us to fall in the brook, do you?" Tommy Fox asked his nearest neighbor. If there was anything that Tommy disliked, it was getting his feet wet.

Major Monkey soon saw that nobody knew what to do.

"Form a long line, two deep!" he directed.

And then there was trouble, because everyone wanted to be in the front rank (as Major Monkey called it) in order to see everything.

After a good deal of jostling and squirming on the part of the company, and much loud talk on the part of Major Monkey, the new army at last stood stretched out in a double line along the pasture-fence.

Major Monkey seemed much pleased as he walked up and down in front of his soldiers. And then he happened to glance up.

There was Mr. Crow, perched on a limb over his head.

"Here, you!" the Major shouted. "Didn't you hear me say 'Fall in?'"

"Certainly!" said Mr. Crow. "But I'm a general, you know."

"Well, what of that?" the Major snapped. "So are all these people generals! You didn't think—did you?—that I'd have anybody in my army that wasn't at least a general?"

For a wonder, Mr. Crow said never a word. He was angry. But he didn't want to be left out of the army. So he decided that he had better obey. And he flapped down and took his place just in front of the front rank.

"You mustn't stand there!" Major Monkey said to him severely. "You're late falling in. There's no place left for you. So you'll have to stand behind all the others."

That was just a little more than old Mr. Crow could bear.

"I'll do nothing of the sort!" he squawked. "And I must say that this is shabby treatment to receive from an old friend."

Major Monkey certainly didn't want any trouble right at the beginning. So he hastened to soothe Mr. Crow's wounded feelings.

"Look here," he said to the old gentleman, "if I were you I shouldn't care to be a common general."

"What else can I be?" asked Mr. Crow with a hopeful gleam in his eye.

"You can be the cook," the Major suggested. "There are dozens of generals; but you'd be the only cook, you see."

Mr. Crow rather liked that idea.

"I accept your offer," he said somewhat stiffly. And then he marched down the line and took his place behind it.

Major Monkey breathed a sigh of relief. He was glad that the trouble had proved no worse. And now he turned once more to inspect the crowd of generals that was to make up his army.

"Here, you!" he said suddenly, pointing to a brownish gentleman at one end of the front rank. "What's your name?"

"Rusty Wren!" was the meek reply.

"Don't stick your tail up in the air like that!" Major Monkey cried. "You're spoiling the looks of the whole army."

Rusty Wren replied that it was very hard for him to keep his tail down for longer than a few moments at a stretch.

"I don't believe I'll be in the army," he announced. "Probably my wife is wondering where I am this moment. So I'm going home." And thereupon he flew away toward Farmer Green's dooryard, where he lived.

"Well, we're rid of him, anyhow," said Major Monkey. And then he noticed something else that wasn't as it should have been.

"Here, you!" he called to Peter Mink. "Pull in your neck! It's too long! It sticks out and spoils the looks of the whole army."

Now, Peter Mink was a rude fellow. And he made such a rude reply that Major Monkey discharged him on the spot.

"Go away!" he cried. "We don't want any rowdies in our army."

XI

War in the Woods

Although Major Monkey had ordered him out of the army, Peter Mink declared that he wasn't going till he was ready to leave.

"Very well," said the Major easily. "You may stay here; and we'll go."

But Peter Mink was an obstinate fellow. The moment the army started to move, he went along with it. And what was worse, he insisted on walking right behind Major Monkey, and trying to strut just as the Major did.

Some of the generals couldn't help snickering. And of course Major Monkey couldn't overlook such behavior.

"Order in the ranks!" he shouted as fiercely as he knew how.

The generals stopped tittering at once. For a minute or two everybody marched on in silence. And then the cry, "Halt!" rang suddenly out.

The generals all stopped. Major Monkey stopped, too. And his face seemed more wrinkled than ever as he looked every general in the face.

Naturally, that took some time, for there were several dozens of them.

"Who shouted 'Halt?'" the Major asked at last.

But nobody knew. At least, nobody answered. And there was a good deal of low talking and craning of necks. For some reason or other, everybody peered at Peter Mink. But he stared straight ahead in the most innocent fashion.

Major Monkey said nothing more. But he walked behind the army and picked up a stick.

"Forward, march!" he commanded then. And as the army moved on, he continued to walk in the rear, just behind old Mr. Crow.

Soon the cry, "Halt!" sounded again. And as soon as he heard it, Major Monkey threw his stick with great force and caught Peter Mink neatly in the back of his head. Peter Mink toppled over where he stood.

"There!" Major Monkey remarked. "He won't bother us any more to-day." And before the army had stopped gasping, he marched it forward again, leaving Peter Mink stretched upon the ground.

Some of the generals objected, and said that they thought that Peter Mink ought to be looked after.

But Major Monkey told them that they were in the army, and that it was war, and they must expect even worse things to happen.

Now, Jimmy Rabbit was a tender-hearted chap. He couldn't bear the thought of leaving even a rascal like Peter Mink wounded and alone.

"I think you ought to send the cook back to take care of him," Jimmy told Major Monkey.

At that, Mr. Crow—who was the cook—spoke up and said that he was going to stay with the army.

"I don't see," he said, "how you could get along without me. An army without a cook is as good as lost."

Major Monkey promptly agreed with Mr. Crow.

"Certainly we mustn't get lost," he said. "If we were lost, the enemy never could find us. And we might wander about in the woods for years and years."

His remarks made some of the generals a bit uneasy. And one of them—a soldier called Billy Woodchuck—announced that he would have to be leaving.

XII

Over and Under

When Billy Woodchuck talked about leaving the army, Major Monkey became greatly excited. He muttered something under his breath aboutdeserters, and shooting them at sunrise. And he strutted up to Billy Woodchuck and asked him what he meant by quitting the army without permission.

Though Billy Woodchuck hung his head, he insisted that he must go home.

"I have an engagement," he explained, "to stand guard in the clover-patch, while my father and some other old gentlemen feast on clover-tops."

"Are they expecting an attack?" Major Monkey inquired, pricking up his ears.

"Of course not!" said Billy Woodchuck. "They're not expecting one, or they would stay safe at home. But you never can tell what old dog Spot is going to do. My father and his friends would be disappointed if I didn't come. They would be angry, too. And just as likely as not I'd be put to bed an hour before sunset. So I shall go home now, whether you give me leave or not."

"Then I'll give you leave—if that's the case," said Major Monkey. "I can't have anybody disobeying orders; so I'll give you leave. And I'll dismiss the army until to-morrow.... The last man over the fence will be shot at sunrise," he added. It seemed as if he was determined to shoot somebody, anyhow.

Well, everyone turned and ran like the wind. Naturally, nobody wanted to be last, after what Major Monkey had said.

It looked, for a few moments, as if the whole army was going to cross the fence at the same instant. But Billy Woodchuck was so unlucky as to step into a hole. He fell head over heels. And by the time he had picked himself up and reached the fence all the rest were safe on the other side of it.

Things looked very dark for Billy Woodchuck—especially when Major Monkey grinned horribly at him between the rails and said:

"Too bad, my boy! But this is war, you know.... Please don't forget the time! To-morrow, at sunrise!"

Billy Woodchuck's heart sank. He wished he had never joined the army. And then an idea came to him. It was such a simple one that it is a wonder he hadn't thought of it instantly. Instead of going over the fence, to everybody's surprise he squirmed under it. And everybody was vastly relieved. Even Major Monkey appeared to be delighted.

"I'm afraid"—he said with a smile—"I'm afraid we'll have to shoot the rest of the army at sunrise, for they went over the fence last."

But Mr. Crow spoke up and said: "Nonsense! The rest of us went over first!"

Major Monkey had to admit that that was true. And he showed plainly that he was disappointed. Although he did not look the least bit cruel, it was clear that he had looked forward to shooting—and the more the merrier.

"It's really a great pity," he said, "that we can't have a shot at somebody."

XIII

The Major Hesitates

Major Monkey's army soon became known far and wide. Its fame reached beyond Pleasant Valley, to the other side of Blue Mountain. And a good many persons who had been in the habit of making excursions into the valley now and then began to think that it was a good place to avoid.

Old Mr. Crow had a good deal to do with spreading the news. He took several long trips, just to tell people that the army was ready — and eager — to fight all strangers.

In fact, the Major said he wished Mr. Crow would mind his own affairs. For how was the army ever going to fight, if all the enemies kept out of its way?

All the generals began to tell one another that Major Monkey was a very brave soldier. And certainly he said nothing to change their opinion of him. He was always telling how much he liked to fight, and complaining that he was only wasting his valuable time in Pleasant Valley.

In a way the Major was right. And probably there never would have been the least trouble if Johnnie Green and his friends hadn't happened to have a picnic in the woods on the same day and in the same spot that the Major had chosen to call his generals together.

Of course, the Major couldn't drill his soldiers with Johnnie Green and a half-dozen other boys on hand to watch. So the generals lurked behind trees and wished that the picnickers would go away.

Meanwhile Major Monkey himself sulked in the tree-tops, hidden high up among the leafy branches, where nobody would be likely to spy him. He watched the boys while they ate their luncheon, which they devoured as soon as they reached the picnic grove. And then he looked on while they played games — hide-and-seek, and duck-on-the-rock, and follow-my-leader, and ever so many others.

Now and then old Mr. Crow flew up and tried to talk with Major Monkey. But the Major had very little to say. And at last Mr. Crow lost all patience with him.

"Are you going to sit here all day and do nothing?" Mr. Crow demanded.

"S-sh!" Major Monkey said. "Do be quiet! Do you want them to hear you?"

"I don't care if they hear me," Mr. Crow cried. "It's plain to me that these boys will stay here all day if they're not driven away."

"No doubt!" Major Monkey agreed, as he plucked a tender shoot off the tree and ate it. "But what can we do?"

"Do!" said Mr. Crow. "What's the army for—I'd like to know—if not to fight?"

Major Monkey's wrinkled face seemed somewhat pale.

"Quite true!" he agreed again. "But I'm not sure we're strong enough to do anything against these ruffians down below. I'm not sure that I can depend on the army in a pinch."

To the Major's great alarm, Mr. Crow squalled with rage.

"You've insulted me!" he shrieked. And he made such a commotion that Major Monkey scampered off, beckoning to Mr. Crow to follow him.

Just as they left, a stone came crashing through the leaves, thrown by some boy who had noticed Mr. Crow's hoarse cries.

And that made Major Monkey run all the faster.

XIV

Throwing Stones

Major Monkey never stopped running until he had gone so far that the voices of the picnickers reached him only faintly.

Old Mr. Crow, who had followed him closely, began to think that the Major was frightened. But he knew he must be mistaken when Major Monkey came to a halt and said: "Now we can talk without disturbing anybody."

So Mr. Crow repeated that in his opinion the Major had insulted him.

"You've just the same as said that I'm a poor soldier!" he declared.

Major Monkey told him that it was not so.

"It's the generals that I can't trust," he explained. "But you are different. You're the cook, you remember. In the midst of a fight, you wouldn't be expected to cook."

"Then my part would be to do nothing at all?" Mr. Crow inquired.

"Exactly!" Major Monkey cried. "And I've no doubt that you'd be a great success."

Old Mr. Crow always liked praise. And of course the Major's remark pleased him. It made him all the more eager, too, to see the army attack Johnnie Green and his friends.

"Let's go back," said Mr. Crow, "and drive those boys out of the picnic grove!"

But Major Monkey shook his head.

"I don't want to lose my army," he said. "And besides we haven't any guns."

"You can throw stones, can't you?" Mr. Crow asked him.

"Oh, yes!" said the Major.

"Well, then—if I were you I'd get some stones down by the brook and go straight back to the grove and hurl them at the enemy."

He said so much more that at last Major Monkey yielded. And a little later he crept back through the tree-tops with all the stones he could carry.

Hidden high above the heads of the picnic party, Major Monkey gave several short whistles. "The attack!" he whispered to old Mr. Crow, who had returned with him to see the fun.

"Hullo!" Johnnie Green shouted, stopping short in the midst of a game of leapfrog. "Who's up there?" And he peered into the greenery above.

Nobody seemed to know the answer to his question. Certainly there was nobody missing from the picnic party.

"I wonder if it's Red Head!" said Johnnie. "You remember he said he couldn't come because he had work to-day. But he must have sneaked over here ahead of us and climbed a tree."

The words were scarcely out of Johnnie Green's mouth when a small stone plunged down from the trees and struck one of his great toes. Being barefooted, Johnnie Green let out a yell.

"Ouch!" he cried. "It's Red Head! There's no doubt about it."

If anybody else had any doubts, they faded quickly when a small shower of stones descended.

"Stop that!" the boys began to shout. "Come down!" And they threatened Red Head with terrible punishments.

Of course, Major Monkey was delighted. He knew that his army of generals could see—and hear—everything. And after he had thrown his last stone he felt so bold that he slipped down upon a lower limb, which gave him a better view of the picnic ground.

One of the boys caught a glimpse of a queer figure above him. And with a shriek he turned and fled.

His companions looked at him in wonder. And Johnnie Green couldn't imagine what had happened, when his staring eyes beheld the Major hanging from a bough over his head.

"It's a monkey!" Johnnie Green gasped. "Where in the world could he have come from?"

XV

The Retreat

Major Monkey quite enjoyed the amazement of the picnickers. And he did two very odd things, for the commander of an army: first he took off his red cap and made a low bow to Johnnie Green and his mates; and next he swung off the limb of the tree and hung by his tail and one hand.

The boys whooped with delight.

"Let's catch him!" Johnnie Green cried. And then he shouted to the boy who had run away, and who stood a good, safe distance off, looking back and wondering what was going on. "Hi, Bill! It's a monkey!" Johnnie bellowed.

Bill came running back at top speed.

"We're going to catch him," said Johnnie Green.

"How're we going to do that?" asked the boy who had been frightened and run away and come back.

Nobody answered him, for at that moment one of the youngsters flung a butternut at the Major, who caught the missile deftly and shot it back again.

A howl of delight from the ground below greeted the Major's ears.

"Let's stone him!" somebody cried.

But Johnnie Green said, "No! We don't want to hurt him. We'll climb the tree and get him."

His friends agreed that that was the better way, after all. And one after another they began to shin up the tree where Major Monkey was still cutting his queer capers. The boys had no sooner started to climb after him than the Major gave a shrill whistle. He was calling for help. But there was not a general in sight anywhere.

He could see not a single one of his whole army, except the cook, old Mr. Crow. And even he flapped away to a neighboring tree-top. As Mr. Crow

37

remarked afterward, since he had to do nothing, he thought he could do it much better if he wasn't too near.

Major Monkey began to chatter. And Mr. Crow always declared that the Major trembled.

There is no doubt that he was alarmed. He scrambled to the very top of the tree, while the boys went up, up, up—until at last Major Monkey gave a scream and jumped into another—and smaller—tree, the top of which was far below him.

He plunged, sprawling, through the leafy boughs until he managed to seize a branch and steady himself. Then he was off like a squirrel. And long before the boys had reached the ground again Major Monkey was far away in the woods.

Mr. Crow took good care not to lose sight of Major Monkey. And when the Major at last stopped, panting, and slipped down to the ground to have a drink out of the brook, old Mr. Crow promptly joined him.

"Aha!" said Mr. Crow. "You were scared. You ran away!"

The Major wiped his mouth on the back of his hand and looked at Mr. Crow uneasily.

"I came away—yes!" he said.

Mr. Crow snorted.

"A fine soldier you are!" he cried scornfully. "You aren't brave enough to lead an army. I should think you'd be ashamed."

Major Monkey seemed pained. He said it hurt him to have Mr. Crow say such cruel things.

"It's plain," said he, "that you don't know much about an army, in spite of all I've tried to teach you. Of course I had to leave. I'm the leader of the army; and I must keep out of danger. So when the generals failed to come to my rescue when I whistled for help there was nothing I could do except retreat."

For a long time Mr. Crow was silent.

"You were scared, anyway," he remarked at last.

"I wasn't!" the Major protested.

"You were!" said Mr. Crow. "You were! You were! You were!"

Of course he was very ill-mannered. But Major Monkey was too polite to tell him so. Instead, he picked up a smooth stone out of the brook and threw it at Mr. Crow's head.

The old gentleman hopped aside just in time. And without waiting to dispute any further, he tore off as fast as he could go.

"Now who's scared?" Major Monkey called after him.

But old Mr. Crow did not stop to answer.

XVI

The Major's Trouble

After Major Monkey fled from Johnnie Green and his friends in the picnic grove, his generals declared that they wanted no leader that ran away from the enemy. And since they couldn't agree on anyone else to take the Major's place, they disbanded.

So Major Monkey lost his army. But the loss did not seem to trouble him greatly. He was almost too cheerful. And his neighbors even claimed that his spirits rose higher each day.

There is no doubt that the Major felt very gay. He was fast losing the lean and hungry look he had had when he first appeared in Pleasant Valley. And he became freer than ever as to manners.

Nobody else could go about the woods with any comfort, because one never knew when he would have to dodge a stone. For Major Monkey liked nothing better than making a body jump—unless it was bowling someone over when he failed to jump soon enough.

In time the forest-folk grew quite weary of that sport. And they began to tell one another that something would have to be done to put an end to Major Monkey's stone-throwing.

But nobody could suggest any way to cure Major Monkey of his unpleasant habit. And at last Mr. Crow went to Aunt Polly Woodchuck and asked her if she couldn't give the Major an herb of some sort to eat, which would make him stop wanting to pelt every head he saw.

But Aunt Polly replied that it wasn't possible.

"The trouble with Major Monkey," she said, "is that he eats too much as it is. And if I gave him still more food he would only throw more stones at you."

Mr. Crow exclaimed that he didn't want that to happen.

"Then you'll have to make the Major eat less," said Aunt Polly Woodchuck. "On what sort of fare is he living at present?" she inquired.

Mr. Crow answered that he wasn't quite sure, but he thought Major Monkey fed for the most part on cowbirds' eggs.

Aunt Polly Woodchuck shook her head.

"That's not possible," she cried. "There aren't enough Cowbirds' eggs in Pleasant Valley to make anybody so fat as the Major is getting. Unless I'm mistaken, he's taking the eggs of a good many others besides Cowbirds."

Mr. Crow became greatly excited.

"Then he's a thief!" he squawked. "Major Monkey is an egg thief!" And he flapped away across the pasture in a fine rage, to tell everybody what Aunt Polly Woodchuck had said.

A little later in the day Major Monkey began to notice that a good many of his neighbors looked at him very coldly. The birds, especially, glared at him as if they were actually angry. And wherever he went they set up a loud twittering. Some of them even flew at his head and tried to peck him as they darted past.

At first he couldn't imagine what was the matter. But before the day was done Jasper Jay let him know what made the bird people angry.

"You're a sneak-thief!" Jasper told the Major bluntly. "We've found at last what makes you so fat. You've been stealing eggs from every nest in the woods!"

"Tut! Tut!" said Major Monkey. "When a lazy Cowbird lays an egg in somebody else's nest, the owner ought to be grateful to me for taking the egg out and eating it."

"It's not that," Jasper Jay replied. "The trouble is, you've taken all kinds of eggs."

"Well, well!" said Major Monkey. "To be sure, I may have made a mistake now and then. But what's an egg or two, more or less, when one has a half-dozen of them?"

XVII

Major Monkey Confesses

Major Monkey seemed surprised when Jasper Jay told him that there wasn't a bird family in the whole valley that felt it could spare a single egg.

"Of course," said Jasper, "nobody cares how many Cowbirds' eggs you eat. The Cowbirds are pests. They are too lazy to build nests of their own. And no respectable bird family likes to have a loutish young Cowbird to bring up with their own children. But you have gone too far. You have been stealing eggs right and left. And the time has come for us to put a stop to your thieving."

A number of Jasper Jay's bird neighbors had gathered around him and Major Monkey while they talked. And they all spoke up and said in good, loud tones that Major Monkey was a villain—and worse.

Anyone might think that for once the Major would have acted the least bit ashamed. But he did not. He had not even the grace to say that he was sorry for making a few "mistakes."

Instead, he stuck his red cap on one side of his head and began dancing something that might have been a jig if it had been faster.

His actions made all the birds very angry. And some of them exclaimed that there was no reason to make merry, so far as they could see.

Major Monkey promptly stopped dancing and looked grieved.

"Perhaps you would dance, too, if you had just had a good meal of eggs," he remarked.

A shriek went up from his listeners. And old Mr. Crow exclaimed loudly: "Put him out! Put Major Monkey out!"

But nobody made a move. And Major Monkey turned to Mr. Crow and said:

"What's wrong? Have I said something I shouldn't?"

"Said!" the old gentleman echoed. "You've not only said a terrible thing; you've done a still worse one! For you've just been stealing eggs again—and you can't deny it."

A great clamor arose all at once.

"Hear! Hear!" Mr. Crow's friends cried.

And Major Monkey had hard work to make himself heard.

"Whose eggs do you think I've been eating?" he asked Mr. Crow.

Not knowing the exact answer to the question, Mr. Crow pretended not to hear it at all. But he looked so slyly at the Major that the Major himself was not deceived. He winked at Mr. Crow and shied a pebble at him.

"I'll tell you, old boy!" the Major cried. "I've been eating hens' eggs."

"Hens' eggs!" everybody repeated after him. "Hens' eggs! Where do you get 'em?"

"At Farmer Green's henhouse, of course," the Major answered. "I've been going there regularly for some time. I find that the eggs are bigger than any I can find in the woods."

"It's no wonder he's getting fat," Jasper Jay murmured as he gazed at Major Monkey.

"You'll have to stop eating so much," Mr. Crow told the Major solemnly. "Aunt Polly Woodchuck says that the reason you throw so many stones is because you overeat and feel in too high spirits."

Major Monkey looked disgusted when he heard that speech.

"Aunt Polly Fiddlesticks!" he jeered. "She doesn't know what she's talking about. Why, the more eggs I eat, the more time I must spend at the henhouse. And while I'm there I can't throw stones here, can I?"

Everybody had to agree with the Major. At least, everybody but Mr. Crow remarked that what he said seemed true.

"Now, friends," said Major Monkey at last, "if there have been any eggs missing from your nests lately you can't blame me."

"Then whom can we blame?" somebody cried.

"I'd hate to say," was Major Monkey's answer. But since he looked straight at Mr. Crow as he spoke, most of the company could not help thinking that the old gentleman was the thief, after all. And when he flew into a rage they felt quite sure he was guilty.

"We always knew Mr. Crow was an old rascal!" they exclaimed.

And so Mr. Crow took himself off. But he soon recovered his good spirits. He was used to being called names. And to tell the truth, he had taken a few eggs now and then — when he thought no one was watching.

XVIII

Planning a Journey

After they learned that Major Monkey was in the habit of going to Farmer Green's henhouse for eggs, the wild folk began to have a better opinion of him once more. So long as he didn't steal birds' eggs they were willing to overlook his stone-throwing — if he didn't throw too many.

Somehow they never seemed to think of Farmer Green's loss. Or if they did, no doubt they thought that he had so many eggs that he wouldn't mind losing a few now and then.

So it happened that Major Monkey found everybody most agreeable — except old Mr. Crow, who never felt the same toward him again.

But Major Monkey did not let Mr. Crow's gruffness trouble him. He had so many other cronies that he frequently remarked that he had never spent a pleasanter summer.

"I've decided" — he told Jolly Robin one day, when he stopped in the orchard to eat an apple — "I've decided to stay right here in Pleasant Valley for the rest of my life."

"My gracious!" Jolly Robin exclaimed. "Then you don't mind cold weather."

Major Monkey asked him what he meant. And it surprised him to learn that all winter long deep snow lay upon the ground, and cold winds blew, and fierce storms often raged.

Though it was a hot summer's day, Major Monkey shivered at the mere mention of such things. And he pulled his red cap further down upon his head.

"If that's the case," he said, "I certainly don't want to spend the winters here.... I don't see how you manage to live through them."

Jolly Robin laughed merrily. "Bless you!" he cried. "I don't stay here the year 'round. As soon as it begins to grow chilly I go South, where it's warm."

Now, Major Monkey looked worried when he heard about the bitter winters in Pleasant Valley. His queer face had screwed itself into even more wrinkles than it usually wore. But as soon as Jolly Robin spoke of going to a warmer place, the Major brightened at once.

"I'm going South too!" he cried. "And if you've no objection we'll travel together."

Jolly Robin said that nothing would please him more.

"I shall be glad to go with you — if my wife doesn't object," he assured the Major.

"Oh! She won't mind," said Major Monkey. "She can go with us. We'll make up a party.... She'll be lucky to go anywhere with such a famous traveller as I am."

Jolly Robin said somewhat doubtfully that he hoped Mrs. Robin would accept their plan. And then he dashed Major Monkey's high hopes by remarking, "Of course, we always fly when we go South."

The Major's face fell. He looked careworn and unhappy again.

"I don't know how to fly," he faltered. "But if you'll fly low, and slowly enough, perhaps I can run through the tree-tops fast enough to keep up with you. I hope it isn't a long trip," he added somewhat anxiously.

"It's about a thousand miles," Jolly Robin told him.

XIX

The Major's Scheme

"I never can run a thousand miles through the tree-tops," Major Monkey told Jolly Robin in a tone of great disappointment. "I don't see how I can spend the winter in the South; and I certainly don't want to stay here, if it's as cold as you say." The poor Major looked so glum that Jolly Robin was sorry for him.

"Can't you get a ride?" he asked.

"I could ride a horse, if I had one," Major Monkey replied.

"That's not a bad idea," Jolly Robin said. "But I'm afraid you'd have trouble finding a horse. Farmer Green would scarcely care to spare one of his horses for so long a trip."

"Well, I could ride a dog," said Major Monkey. "There's that dog at the farmhouse — old Spot, as you call him. Surely Farmer Green wouldn't mind if I rode him away, for he's nothing but a nuisance."

"Why don't you ask Farmer Green?" Jolly Robin suggested.

But Major Monkey shook his head.

"No!" he said. "No! I don't want to do that yet. Before I speak to Farmer Green I prefer to make sure that old dog Spot is easy to ride on."

Jolly Robin looked puzzled. His mouth fell open. And for a few moments he stared at Major Monkey without saying a word.

When he finally spoke, it was to ask Major Monkey how he was going to find out what he wanted to know about old dog Spot.

"There's only one way," said Major Monkey. "There's only one way; and that's to ride him and see."

Jolly Robin thought what a bold fellow Major Monkey was. He entirely forgot the Major's flight from the picnic grove. Riding a dog was such a feat as Jolly Robin himself would never, never attempt. And he was sure that if Major Monkey really undertook it there could be no doubt of his bravery.

"How do you know" — Jolly asked the Major timidly — "how do you know that old dog Spot will let you ride him?"

"Don't you worry about that!" Major Monkey cried lightly, as he swaggered along a limb of the apple tree where they were talking. "Leave that to me."

And Jolly Robin thought what a stout heart beat beneath Major Monkey's red coat, and how fine it was to be one of his friends.

"I should like to see you when you first ride old Spot," said Jolly Robin.

"Delighted, I'm sure!" Major Monkey cried.

"And I hope you've no objection to my bringing my wife along, too."

Major Monkey was not so sure that he would care to have Mrs. Robin for an onlooker.

"Women are likely to be timid," he remarked. "They sometimes scream at the wrong time. And if your wife happened to cry out just as I was about to drop on old Spot's back, he might jump. And that would spoil everything."

Jolly Robin decided that Major Monkey knew best.

"We'll keep this affair a secret," he whispered.

The Major nodded.

"And now" — Jolly Robin asked him — "now where and when are you going to ride old Spot?"

Shutting his eyes tightly, Major Monkey wrinkled his low forehead until Jolly Robin began to fear that he was in great pain.

"Are you ill?" Jolly asked him.

"No!" said the Major. "I was only thinking. And it seems to me that the other end of the orchard, toward the farmhouse, would be the best place to begin my ride.... As for the time," he added, "that will be when old Spot happens to come that way."

"I'll be there, whenever that may be," Jolly Robin assured him.

XX

A Fast Ride

For once Mrs. Robin had reason to complain that her husband did not do his share of the work. Jolly Robin would spend most of his time at the further end of the orchard, talking with "that good-for-nothing Major Monkey," to use Mrs. Robin's own words.

Whenever she flew over to speak to her husband, the Major was most polite to her, never failing to take off his cap and ask after her health. But Mrs. Robin had little to say to him. She had, however, a great deal to say to Jolly Robin. But no matter how much she urged him to stop idling and come home and help her look after their big family, Jolly insisted that he and the Major "had business to attend to."

At last, when Mrs. Robin gave up in despair, Jolly began to feel somewhat uncomfortable. And he tried to get Major Monkey to go and ask old dog Spot to come to the orchard, instead of waiting there uncertainly for days and days.

But Major Monkey would not consent to such a move. He was quite firm.

"I don't want to ask old Spot to give me a ride," he explained.

"Then how do you ever expect to get one?" Jolly asked him anxiously.

"Oh, there's a way!" was the Major's mysterious reply. And that was all he would say.

The longer Jolly Robin waited to see the fun, the more excited he became, and the more Major Monkey seemed to enjoy himself.

"Old dog Spot ought to be here soon," the Major kept saying. "I can see him now. No! I'm mistaken."

Jolly Robin had so many disappointments that one morning when the Major cried out that at last old Spot was actually crawling through the fence, and would be in the orchard in about a minute and a half, Jolly couldn't believe him.

It was true, nevertheless. To Jolly's delight, old dog Spot came darting in and out among the apple trees, with his nose close to the ground. He was following a trail made by Tommy Fox, who had visited the henhouse the night before. And he was so intent on what he was doing that never once did he glance up into the apple trees, where Major Monkey and Jolly Robin were watching him.

Major Monkey dropped quickly down to a low-hanging limb. And as luck had it, Tommy Fox's trail led old dog Spot right under the tree where the Major waited, hanging gracefully by his tail and one hand.

As old Spot passed below him, Major Monkey loosened his hold on the limb and dropped squarely upon old Spot's back.

The moment he landed, the Major dug his fingers into Spot's long fur and hung on grimly. And at the same instant old dog Spot leaped high into the air and let out a frenzied yelp.

Jolly Robin was glad that his wife was not present, for he knew that the sight, and the sound too, could not have failed to terrify her.

Old Spot seemed almost out of his mind. For a few moments the poor fellow tore about the orchard in wide circles, hoping in vain that he might shake that strange load off his back.

But he soon saw that his rider clung to him like a burr. And wheeling suddenly, Spot shot like a streak out of the orchard and flew across the meadow.

Just before he disappeared behind a high knoll Major Monkey turned his face over his shoulder and looked behind. Then, holding on with one hand, with the either he waved his red cap at Jolly Robin.

The next moment Jolly saw the Major and his strange steed no more.

"They headed straight for the river!" Jolly exclaimed. And he felt so worried about his friend the Major that though he went home at once, his wife complained that his mind wasn't on his work and that he was more bother than help to her.

Some time later Major Monkey limped back to his home in the haystack, dripping wet. His fine coat was torn. And he had lost his red cap.

When Jolly Robin saw him he asked the Major if he had had a good ride.

"Well," said Major Monkey, "it was a good one; but it was too fast. If I started to travel south on old dog Spot's back I'd reach my journey's end before you had gone half way."

"Dear me!" said Jolly Robin. "Then we can't travel together after all."

XXI

A Sweet Tooth

After his ride on old dog Spot, Major Monkey went to the henhouse for eggs even oftener than he had gone before.

Perhaps he had become fonder of eggs. Or perhaps he had become bolder. Anyhow, he noticed that old dog Spot gave him a wide berth. Whenever old Spot saw him he tucked his tail between his legs and ran, yelping, into the house.

Now, Johnnie Green soon discovered that something — or somebody — was frightening old Spot almost every day. And having nothing else to do one morning, he made up his mind that he would watch and see what happened. So he climbed to the cupola on top of the big barn. And there he stayed for a long time, keeping a sharp eye on old Spot as he wandered about the farm buildings.

It was a good while before anything happened. But Johnnie Green did not mind that. He had brought plenty of cookies to munch. And he pretended that he was a sailor in the crow's nest of a ship, on the lookout for a sail.

After a while he almost forgot what he was really doing. He was leaning far out of the cupola, shading his eyes with one hand, and stuffing a cookie into his mouth with the other, and gazing off across the meadow, when all at once he heard old Spot yelping.

That sound brought Johnnie to his senses. And glancing down, he saw Spot tearing across the barnyard, making for the woodshed door in great bounds. And behind him, perched on the roof of the henhouse, Johnnie saw a familiar figure.

"It's the monkey again!" Johnnie Green cried. And he clambered quickly to the ground.

But when he reached the henhouse Major Monkey had fled. Johnnie could see his red coat flickering among the leaves in the orchard. But he knew it was useless to follow.

Although Major Monkey was aware that Johnnie Green had seen him again, he did not stop visiting the henhouse. To be sure, he became somewhat more wary. He never went inside the henhouse for eggs without first looking around carefully, to make sure that Johnnie Green wasn't watching him. And for a time the Major kept an eye out for traps.

He saw nothing of the sort anywhere. But one day when he leaped to the window-sill of the henhouse he was delighted to find a lump of maple sugar, which some one had carelessly left there.

At least, that was what the Major supposed. And with something a good deal like a chuckle he ate the dainty greedily. It was the first bit of sugar he had tasted since he came to Pleasant Valley. And Major Monkey was very fond of sweets.

Johnnie Green, or his father, or the hired man seemed all at once to grow terribly careless with maple sugar. The Major hardly ever visited the henhouse without finding a lump somewhere. And if his liking for eggs hadn't brought him thither daily, his taste for sugar would have been enough to make him continue his visits.

At last there came a day when Major Monkey discovered a thick pitcher on the henhouse floor. A chain was looped through its handle and nailed to the wall.

The Major grinned when he saw the chain.

"They don't want this pitcher to run away," he said to himself.

Being of a most curious turn of mind, he looked into the pitcher. And then he promptly thrust in a hand.

There was a good-sized lump of sugar inside. And Major Monkey's fingers closed upon it greedily.

His queer face wrinkled with annoyance when he found that he could not withdraw his hand. Empty, it could easily have slipped through the mouth of the pitcher. But with the sugar clutched in it, his hand stuck fast.

XXII

Caught!

Though Major Monkey tugged and tugged, he couldn't pull his hand out of the pitcher.

To be sure, if he had let go of the lump of maple sugar he might have withdrawn his hand easily enough.

But the Major loved sweets too dearly to loosen his hold on any such toothsome morsel — except to pop it into his mouth.

So he struggled and fretted. He even tried to break the pitcher by knocking it against the floor.

It might as well have been made of iron, it was so strong. And the Major only succeeded in hurting his own hand.

Of course he made a great racket. And the hens, who had become used to his more stealthy visits, began to flutter and squawk. They made such an uproar at last that Major Monkey wanted to hurl the pitcher at them. But he couldn't do that, with his hand stuck inside it. And besides, the pitcher was chained fast to the wall of the henhouse.

And right there lay the Major's greatest trouble. If the pitcher hadn't been fastened he would have run off on three legs, to the woods, where he might have tried in peace and quiet to get at the sugar inside it.

On the whole, Major Monkey spent a most unhappy quarter of an hour in the henhouse. And the worst moment of all came when the window dropped with a loud bang.

Then the sound of steps on the threshold made the Major turn his head.

There stood Farmer Green with a broad smile on his face, and Johnnie Green with his mouth wide open and his eyes bulging.

And with them was a dark-skinned man, short, and with rings in his ears, and a bright neckerchief tied about his throat.

"Aha-a!" cried the little man. "Look-a da monk! He greed-a boy!" And picking Major Monkey up in his arms, jug and all, he patted him fondly, saying, "Ah-a! Bad-a boy! He run-a da way from da ol' man, no?"

Then—for a soldier—Major Monkey did a strange thing. He began to whimper. But there is no doubt that he was weeping because he was glad, and not because he was sorry.

The little, dark man was his master.

And the Major was very, very fond of him. He knew, suddenly, that he had missed the little man sadly while he roamed about Pleasant Valley.

Though Johnnie Green was staring straight at him, Major Monkey clung to his captor and held his wrinkled face close to the little man's cheek.

"He sorra now!" the little man said to Johnnie Green.

"What's his name?" Johnnie inquired.

"Jocko!" said Major Monkey's master. "Dat nice-a name, eh?"

Johnnie Green thought that it was. And Major Monkey himself appeared to like the sound of it. It was a long time since he had heard it. No one had called him "Jocko" since that day—weeks before—when he had run away from his master, the organ-grinder, in the village.

XXIII

The Major Goes South

Out of one of his pockets the hand-organ man pulled a stout collar, from which dangled a long, thin chain. And Major Monkey made no protest when his master buckled the collar about his neck.

To tell the truth, the Major appeared to like being a captive. He was enjoying, especially, the maple sugar which the hand-organ man had turned out of the pitcher for him.

At the farmhouse, a little later, Major Monkey went through all his tricks for Johnnie Green and the rest of the family. Though he had once told Mr. Crow that he never wanted to hear the sound of a hand-organ again, the music that his master ground out while he himself capered about seemed to him the sweetest he had ever heard.

Of the Major's audience, the most astonished of all sat, unnoticed, in a tree in the dooryard and listened and looked on as if he could scarcely believe his eyes.

This one was Jolly Robin. And when, at length, the organ-grinder looped the long chain over his arm, slung the organ over his back, and went toiling up the road, with Major Monkey perched on top of the hand-organ, Jolly Robin had a very queer feeling. He flew down and alighted upon Farmer Greene's fence and trilled a quavering good-by. Major Monkey stood up and made a low bow to him. "He's going South, after all!" Jolly Robin said to himself. If that was so, old dog Spot must have been glad of it. Anyhow, he dashed out of the dooryard and ran a little way up the road, growling and barking, and telling Major Monkey exactly what he thought of him.

The Major seemed to enjoy old Spot's farewell. He danced up and down, and pulled back his arm, as if to throw something at Spot. But he changed his mind. He had a red apple, which Johnnie Green had given him. And instead of wasting it on old dog Spot, the Major took a bite out of it then and there.

58

Old Spot had trotted back to the farmhouse, looking very brave, in spite of the scolding Johnnie Green gave him. And Major Monkey was busily engaged with his apple, when he heard a sound that made him look up.

"Caw! Caw!" It was old Mr. Crow, whose keen eyes had caught sight of the hand-organ man plodding along with his precious load. Major Monkey whistled. And just for a moment, as he watched Mr. Crow sailing lazily overhead, he almost wished that he hadn't been quite so fond of sugar. For he knew that he could no longer wander through Pleasant Valley wherever his fancy led him.

But the hand-organ man began singing a merry song. And Major Monkey liked it so well that before he had gone a mile he wouldn't have turned back for anything. Now that his play-time had come to an end, he was eager to journey on, wherever his master might take him.

For Major Monkey—as he had told Mr. Crow in the beginning—was a great traveller.

Milton Keynes UK
Ingram Content Group UK Ltd.
UKHW040748181023
430769UK00004B/141